INSPIRELAND
School Stories
of Everyday Boy Heroes

An Awesome Collection of Inspiring Short Tales for Boys That Build Courage, Perseverance, Kindness, Integrity, and Gratitude (Motivational Books for Kids)

Grace Ann Grow

To the everyday heroes—

This book is dedicated to the boys who dare to dream big, stand tall, and embrace courage in their own unique ways. Whether you're navigating challenges, standing up for what's right, or simply giving your best each day, you are the heart and soul of these stories.

Always remember, being a hero doesn't require perfection. It's about demonstrating kindness, resilience, and bravery, no matter the size of the moment.

Keep shining your light—you hold the power to change the world, starting today.

With deep gratitude and admiration,
Grace Ann Grow

Contents

Introduction

Hey there, adventurer!

Have you ever felt like being a hero is something only superheroes in movies can do? Maybe you've wondered if you're strong enough, brave enough, or clever enough to handle the challenges life throws at you. Here's a secret: real heroes aren't born—they're made through everyday actions, big and small.

In school hallways, on playgrounds, or even during quiet moments at home, boys like you face situations that test their courage and kindness. Maybe you've had to stand up to a bully, face your fears, or lend a hand when someone needed help. *However, there are moments when you find yourself questioning, "What should I do?" How can I make a difference?*

That's where this book comes in. *INSPIRELAND* is filled with captivating tales of boys, similar to you, who encounter extraordinary circumstances. Whether it's defending a friend, standing tall against fears, or using their talents to help others, these boys prove that being a hero doesn't mean being perfect. It means trying, learning, and growing.

In these pages, you'll meet Timmy, who discovers that courage isn't about not being scared but taking action anyway. You'll cheer for Miguel, who finds strength in teamwork on the baseball field, and admire Sunwoo, who sacrifices a big dream to care for his family. These tales of bravery, kindness, and resilience will demonstrate the diversity of heroes.

Why should you trust me with these stories? Well, I've been where you are, wondering how to handle tricky situations. I've spent years listening to and sharing stories of kids who've faced challenges and triumphed. And I believe in the incredible potential inside every boy—including you. Writing this book isn't just a job for me; it's my way of inspiring the next generation of everyday heroes.

Here's my promise: as you read this book, you'll find the courage to tackle your own challenges. You'll learn to see problems as opportunities to grow stronger and kinder. And you'll discover how small acts of bravery can make a big difference in your life—and the lives of those around you.

Every day is a chance to become someone's hero, even if that hero is just a better version of yourself. If you keep putting it off, you might miss out on the amazing adventures waiting for you.

So, what are you waiting for? Dive into these stories and uncover the secrets of real-life heroism. You might just find that the next exciting adventure is your own.

Are you ready? Let's go!

The Volcano of Courage

A New Beginning

Timmy James stands outside the tall gates of Woodgrove Middle School, his heart pounding like a bass drum. On his first day in fifth grade, his stomach is tense. His big brother always tells him that middle school is a jungle—a wild place where only the strong survive. And Timmy? Well, he's not sure he's strong enough.

But Timmy isn't the type to back down. Neither today nor ever will he back down. He straightens his backpack straps and takes a deep breath. "Alright, here goes nothing," he mutters to himself.

Inside, the hallway is a frenzy of kids moving in every direction. Groups of friends laugh, lockers clang shut, and the constant buzz of chatter fills the air. Timmy feels like a tiny boat lost in a stormy sea. He spots his best friend, Leo Sanchez, near their homeroom. Leo, with his wild curly hair and an easygoing grin, always seems to have everything under control.

"Timmy, you made it!" Leo waves him over. "Ready to conquer fifth grade?"

Timmy shrugs, attempting to maintain composure. "As ready as I'll ever be."

The Volcano Challenge

Their first class is science with Mr. Gruber, a towering man with a booming voice and a permanent frown. "Settle down, class," he commands. "Today, we're starting our first big project—The Volcano Challenge. You will work in pairs to create a model volcano. The winning team will have their project displayed at the science fair next month!"

Timmy's heart races with excitement. Is he going to present a science fair project to the entire school? The idea both excites and terrifies him. He and Leo exchange a quick look, a silent agreement to partner up. They both love a positive challenge, but this one feels... daunting.

After school, they head to Leo's garage, their usual hangout and makeshift lab. "Okay, let's build the most epic volcano this school has ever seen," Leo declares. He pulls out a sketchpad and starts drawing. Timmy watches, nodding along, but his mind drifts. He's not sure a paper-mâché volcano is enough. He wants to make something special to show his brother and others he's not a quiet kid.

"What if...," Timmy says slowly, "we make it explode for real? Like, a legit eruption with smoke and everything?"

Leo's eyes widen. "Dude, that could be awesome. Or a disaster."

"Yeah," Timmy grins, "but wouldn't it be epic either way?"

Experiment Gone Awry

For the next few days, they gather supplies—baking soda, vinegar, and food coloring. But Timmy wants more than just a fizz. He spends hours online, reading about real volcanic eruptions and chemical reactions. Soon, his notebook is filled with scribbles and formulas. Leo looks at him like he's slightly lost his mind, but Timmy doesn't care. He's got a plan.

The following week, they test their first version in Leo's garage. Built from layers of cardboard and plaster, the volcano stands tall, its crater seemingly beckoning them to unleash its fury. Timmy carefully pours in his secret concoction—a mix of dry ice, mentos, and some mysterious powder he bought from the hobby store.

"Ready?" he asks, a spark of excitement in his eyes.

"Ready," Leo says, holding up his phone to record.

Timmy drops in the final ingredient, and for a moment, nothing happens. Leo sighs in disappointment. But then, with a hissing roar, the volcano bursts to life! A plume of white smoke billows out, followed by a red, frothy explosion that sprays everywhere. It's glorious for about three seconds— until the smoke detector starts blaring, and Leo's mom rushes in, eyes wide.

"What in the world are you boys doing?!"

Timmy and Leo quickly wave away the smoke, coughing and laughing. "It worked!" Timmy exclaims.

Leo's mom isn't amused. "Clean up this mess right now, and no more experiments like this in the house!"

The Whisper Campaign

Timmy is still filled with excitement the next day at school. But then he overhears a conversation that brings him crashing down. Jessica Nguyen, the class outlier, whispers, "Did you hear about Timmy and Leo?" "They almost blew up Leo's garage! How lame can you get?"

Timmy's face burns with embarrassment. Maybe he pushed too hard. Maybe he should have stuck with the safe route.

But Leo doesn't seem fazed. "Forget them," he says. "They wouldn't know a cool science project if it hit them in the face. We just need to make sure it's even better next time."

Timmy nods, though doubt still lingers. The next week is tough. Their experiments keep failing, and their project is running out of time. Timmy begins to question whether he has taken on more than he can handle.

A Hero Emerges

Then, on a rainy afternoon, everything changes. Timmy is walking home alone when he hears shouting from the old community park. His curiosity compels him to sneak closer and investigate the situation. Three older boys from the eighth grade—Trevor, Malik, and Scott—have cornered a small sixth-grader, Alex. They're tossing his backpack around, taunting him as he tries desperately to grab it back.

Timmy's heartbeat quickens. He knows he should keep walking. These guys pose a significant threat. But then he sees Alex's face, red and on the brink of tears. Suddenly, Timmy remembers how he felt on his first day—small, scared, out of place.

Something snaps inside him. He doesn't think; he just acts. He charges forward. "Hey! Leave him alone!"

The bullies turn, surprised. Trevor, the ringleader, sneers. "Well, well, if it isn't Timmy 'the Volcano Kid.' What are you gonna do, nerd? Make us a science project?"

Timmy's hands tremble, but he clenches them into fists. "I'm not scared of you, Trevor. Just let him go."

For a moment, there's tense silence. Then, with a roar of laughter, Trevor lunges forward, shoving Timmy to the ground. "You should've stayed out of it!"

But Timmy doesn't back down. He scrambles up, eyes blazing with determination. "You think you're tough picking on a sixth-grader? How about facing someone your own size?"

The other kids at the park are starting to gather around, forming a circle. Some are filming with their phones. Trevor's bravado fades a bit as he realizes all eyes are on him.

Malik steps forward, but before he can do anything, Leo bursts onto the scene, dragging along Mrs. Henderson, the school's toughest gym teacher.

"What's going on here?" She barks, her voice enough to make even the boldest kids freeze.

Trevor and his gang scatter like rats. Mrs. Henderson glares after them but then turns to Timmy and Alex. "Are you boys okay?"

Timmy nods, a bit shaky, but he feels a warmth spreading through his chest—a sense of pride.

A New Reputation

The story rapidly spreads throughout the school. Timmy "The Volcano Kid" stood up to Trevor and his gang. Kids he's never talked to before give him high-fives in the halls. Even Jessica Nguyen, who always thought she was better than everyone else, looks at him with newfound respect.

Leo pats him on the back. "Dude, you were epic. Like a real-life hero."

Timmy grins, feeling a confidence he's never known before. "I guess I just decided I wasn't going to be scared anymore."

The Grand Finale

When the day of the Volcano Challenge finally arrives, Timmy and Leo's project is ready. This time, they've perfected their formula, using everything they've learned. When it's their turn, the whole room is buzzing with anticipation.

Timmy looks at Leo, and Leo nods. They trigger the eruption, and the volcano springs to life with a perfect blend of smoke, lava, and a few harmless sparks that light up the room. The crowd erupts in cheers.

Mr. Gruber nods approvingly. "Now that is what I call an eruption! You boys have certainly earned a spot in the science fair."

Afterward, Alex comes up to Timmy. "Thanks for standing up for me," he says, his voice quiet but sincere.

"No problem," Timmy replies with a grin. "Sometimes, you just have to stand up and show them you're not afraid."

As Timmy walks home that day, he realizes something important. It isn't about being the strongest or the smartest. It's about having the courage to stand up for what's right, even when it's hard. It's about taking risks, facing fears, and learning from every mistake. And that, he thinks, is the real adventure.

From that day on, Timmy James isn't just known as "The Volcano Kid"—he's known as the kid who dared to stand up, speak out, and make a difference. And he's pretty sure this is just the beginning of many more brave quests to come.

The Miracle at Westfield

The Heat of the Moment

The sun burns hot above the baseball field, its rays bouncing off the red dirt and freshly chalked white lines, casting long shadows that stretch toward the cheering crowd. A soft breeze rustles through the American flag hanging high above the scoreboard, where the numbers stubbornly refuse to budge in Miguel Rivera's favor. The score reads 6–4, and Miguel's team, the Westfield Warriors, has just one inning left to close the gap. The tension in the air is thick, a mix of anticipation and hope, as if the entire field is holding its breath.

Miguel, a ten-year-old with a wiry frame and an easy smile that masks his nerves, stands near the dugout, his glove clutched tightly in one hand. His heart races as he scans the field, his thoughts swirling with anticipation and a flicker of doubt. He tries to channel the determination he's practiced all season, taking a deep breath to steady himself, but the enormity of the moment—the championship game—lingers in the back of his mind like a drumbeat. His dark hair curls slightly at the edges of his cap, and his deep brown eyes scan the field as if he's trying to memorize every detail of the moment. This is more than a game; it's the championship, the culmination of months of hard work and sacrifice. Around him, the crowd's energy pulses like a heartbeat, loud and steady, rising and falling with every pitch.

"We've got this, guys," Miguel says, his voice quiet but firm, like a steady anchor in the storm. His teammates gather around him, their faces a mix of exhaustion and determination. Most of them are bigger than Miguel, but they listen when he speaks. There's something about him—a calm confidence that makes people believe, even when the odds seem insurmountable.

"Miguel, we need a miracle," says Jordan, the team's star pitcher, wiping sweat off his forehead with the back of his hand. His jersey clings to him, damp from the heat and the pressure. "They've been hitting everything I throw."

"Then we'll make our own miracle," Miguel replies, a small grin tugging at his lips. His voice carries a quiet determination, the kind that doesn't shout but commands attention. He's not just saying it; he means it. He's thinking ahead, his mind already mapping out the moves they need to make.

Rising Through Adversity

Miguel didn't start the season as the team's leader. During one of the early practices, the team was struggling to stay focused in the sweltering heat. Most of the players were sitting under the shade of the dugout, complaining about the drills. However, Miguel remained on the field, performing laps and retrieving stray balls without any requests. When the coach noticed Miguel's effort, he called out, "If you all worked as hard as Miguel, we'd be unstoppable." From that day on, the team's perception of him began to shift. His actions carried more weight than his words, leading his teammates to emulate him. At the tryouts months ago, he'd been the quiet kid who barely spoke a word. He had arrived with an old glove, its leather worn soft from years of backyard games. Some of the other boys even joked that he wouldn't last a week on the field. Miguel smiled and shrugged, letting the comments slide off him like water. What they didn't see was the fire inside him—the determination to prove himself.

Every practice, Miguel hustled harder than anyone else. Miguel remained focused, running extra laps, taking extra swings in the batting cage, and studying the game like a puzzle waiting to be solved, while others laughed and joked between drills. His dedication gradually won over everyone. By midseason, he was the player everyone looked to in tough moments, not because he was the biggest or the fastest, but because he never gave up.

The Turning Point

Back on the field, the Warriors take their positions. Miguel jogs to second base, his favorite spot. From here, he can see everything: the batter's stance, the pitcher's windup, the slight shift of an outfielder ready to sprint. It's a good place to be when you're trying to read the game like a story unfolding in real time.

The Maple Valley Eagles, who are the opposing team, prepare to bat. Their best hitter, a stocky kid named Blake, smirks as he twirls his bat in his hands, his confidence radiating like heat off the field. Miguel's heart pounds, but he focuses on his breathing, steady and slow, grounding himself in the moment.

Jordan winds up and throws. Crack! The stadium echoes with a sharp sound, temporarily silencing the crowd before a collective gasp ripples through the stands. Blake's bat unleashes a ball that slashes through the air like a missile, heading towards right field. Parents and kids alike jump to their feet, shouting encouragement and warnings, their voices blending into a chaotic symphony of tension. The sound of rushing footsteps on the grass and the faint rustle of the wind carry across the field as Malik, the right fielder, dashes toward the ball with laser focus. The crowd gasps, a collective intake of breath. Malik, their right fielder, sprints as if his life is at stake. His legs pump furiously, his eyes locked on the ball. He dives, glove outstretched, and catches the ball just before it hits the ground. The crowd erupts in cheers, their applause rolling like thunder, and Miguel feels a surge of hope ripple through the team.

After two outs, the Warriors take the batting position. Miguel watches as his teammates give it their all, swinging hard and running fast. Sweat drips down their faces, but they don't let up. They manage to load the bases, and now it's Miguel's turn. He grabs his bat, the weight of it familiar and comforting in his hands, and steps up to the plate. The weight of the moment settles on his shoulders, but he doesn't let it crush him. Instead, he remembers his father's words: "The only thing you control is your effort. Give it everything."

The pitcher glares at him, winds up, and throws. The ball whistles through the air, a blur of white. Miguel swings, and the crack of the bat meeting the ball echoes across the field. It's a line drive, fast and low, streaking past the shortstop. Two runners make it home, tying the game. The crowd is on its feet, roaring, their cheers vibrating in Miguel's chest. His heart races as he stands on second base, his grin wide and unstoppable. For a moment, it feels like the world is spinning just for him.

But the inning ends before they can score again. Now it's sudden death. One more run from either team will decide the championship.

The Final Play

The Eagles demonstrate their desperation in every movement. The Warriors' defense holds strong. Miguel dives to catch a grounder, the dirt flying up as he stretches his glove. He flips it to first base just in time. The crowd erupts again, their cheers blending into a single wave of sound that seems to carry the team forward.

As the Warriors take their final turn at bat, Miguel senses the weight of the game shifting. The Eagles' pitcher is tired, his throws losing speed and precision. Miguel leans over to Jordan, whispering a quick plan, his voice steady despite the adrenaline surging through him.

"Think it'll work?" Jordan asks, his eyebrows raised, the uncertainty clear in his voice.

"It has to," Miguel replies, his tone leaving no room for doubt.

Jordan steps up to bat and does exactly what Miguel suggested: he bunts. The ball rolls slowly down the third baseline, wobbling slightly. Jordan sprints for first, his legs churning with everything he has. The pitcher scrambles, lunging for the ball, but his throw is wild. The crowd gasps as the ball sails past first base, and Jordan makes it to second, safe.

Miguel is up next. The crowd tenses up, the tension is palpable. Stepping up to the plate, he grips his bat tightly as a hundred thoughts race through his mind. What if I strike out? What if I let them down? He swallows hard, forcing himself to focus. This isn't just about him—it's about the team, the countless hours of practice, the sacrifices they've all made. He takes a deep breath, imagining his father's voice: "Stay steady, Mijo. Trust your instincts." The noise of the crowd fades, replaced by the steady rhythm of his heartbeat as he locks eyes with the pitcher. Miguel takes a deep breath, gripping the bat tightly. The pitcher throws, and Miguel swings with all his strength. The ball sails into the outfield, high and fast, catching the sunlight as it arcs. Jordan sprints home, his cleats digging into the dirt. The crowd explodes as Jordan slides across the plate, safe. The Warriors win.

Lessons in Leadership

After the game, as the team celebrates, Miguel stands quietly by the dugout, his heart full and his mind replaying the pivotal moments. He recalls the crack of his bat meeting the ball in the final inning, the rush of adrenaline as Jordan slid across the plate, and the roar of the crowd when the Warriors claimed victory. He also thinks of the earlier practices when he stayed late, picking up stray balls and running extra drills, and how those moments built the trust of his teammates. Each memory feels like a piece of a puzzle, coming together to form a picture of triumph earned through determination and teamwork. One of the younger players, a shy boy named Ethan, approaches him, his eyes wide with admiration.

"Miguel, how did you stay so calm?" Ethan inquires, his voice hardly audible above a whisper.

Miguel crouches down to meet Ethan's eyes, a gentle smile on his face. "It's not about being calm all the time. It's about focusing on what you can do and doing your best. That's all anyone can ask for."

Ethan nods, a small smile spreading across his face as if Miguel's words have unlocked something inside him. Miguel ruffles his hair and stands, looking out at the field one last time. Today, he was a hero, not because he hit the ball or made the play, but because he showed his team what it means to never give up.

As the sun sets, painting the sky in shades of orange and pink, Miguel knows this is a moment he'll carry with him forever. And maybe—just maybe—so will everyone else.

Between Dreams and Duty

The First Test

Sunwoo Park stands at the edge of the gymnasium, the buzz of the crowd rattling his nerves. His jet-black hair, slightly tousled from the brisk walk over, frames a face that's both intense and approachable. Dressed in his school's navy hoodie and sneakers scuffed from countless late-night robotics sessions, he has an air of quiet determination. A small, calloused scar on his hand from a soldering mishap hints at his dedication to his craft. Today is the All-City Robotics Expo, an event he's been preparing for months. The sleek, blue robot he designed and built glides beside him, a testament to countless late nights spent sketching blueprints, soldering wires, and coding endless lines of instructions. The air smells like polished floors and fried snacks from the concession stand, and Sunwoo's heart pounds with a mix of anticipation and anxiety.

Then his phone vibrates in his pocket.

His stomach knots as he pulls it out. A text from his older sister, Jiyeon, pops onto the screen: "Dad's fever is worse. Mom's asking if you can come home. She's exhausted."

Sunwoo's fingers hover over the keyboard. He glances back at his robot, then at the competition floor where teams are setting up. The announcer's voice crackles through the speakers, calling participants to prepare for the first round.

He types back, "I'll try."

His mind is filled with excitement. Winning this competition could lead to scholarships, recognition, and a significant step towards his dream of becoming an engineer. Ever since he was a kid, Sunwoo has been fascinated by machines. He remembers the day his father brought home a broken radio from the thrift store and challenged him to fix it. They spent hours together at the kitchen table, his father's patient guidance and encouraging words sparking a love for problem-solving. That memory fuels him now, reminding him why this path matters so much—not just for himself, but to honor the bond he shares with his dad. However, his father's health has been declining at home, and the family is struggling to maintain stability. His mom runs a small laundromat and barely gets enough sleep. Jiyeon works part-time to help pay bills while juggling college classes.

Sunwoo's been the "happy middle kid," the one who rarely causes trouble. But right now, he feels split in two.

A Difficult Decision

"Hey, Sunwoo!" A familiar voice jolts him from his thoughts. It's Miles, his best friend and team partner, waving enthusiastically. Miles's dark brown curls bounce as he jogs over. "Ready to crush it?"

"Yeah," Sunwoo says, forcing a grin. But the weight in his chest doesn't budge.

As the first round begins, Sunwoo's hands move automatically, guiding their robot through a maze of obstacles. The crowd cheers when it completes the final challenge in record time. Miles fist-bumps him. "We're dominating! Next round's ours for sure."

But Sunwoo barely hears him. His phone vibrates again. Jiyeon has sent another message: "Mom's been up all night. We need help."

His chest tightens. He excuses himself, weaving through the bustling gym to a quiet corner by the water fountain. He calls home, and his mother answers on the first ring.

"Sunwoo? Are you busy?" Her voice is strained, and he can hear the faint sound of coughing in the background. "I hate to ask, but—"

"I can come home," he blurts out, cutting her off.

She hesitates. "No, no, you've worked so hard for today. I… We'll manage."

But Sunwoo knows better. His mom always says they'll manage, even when things are falling apart. He's seen her push through exhaustion, smile through frustration, and shoulder burdens she never complains about.

He clenches his jaw. What kind of son would he be if he let her keep doing that alone?

Leaving It Behind

Back in the gym, Miles is adjusting the robot for the second round. "You've got to see the other teams," he says, nodding toward the competitors. "We've totally got this."

Sunwoo hesitates, then takes a deep breath. "Miles," he begins carefully, "something's come up at home. I might have to leave."

Miles freezes. "Wait, what? Now? Dude, the finals are in an hour!"

"I know. But my dad's sick, and my mom needs help."

Miles's eyebrows knit together. "Can't it wait? Could you please wait a little longer? We've been prepping for this all year. You said this was your dream."

"It is," Sunwoo says quietly. "But my family… they come first."

The disappointment on Miles's face stings, and he stands silent for a moment, his shoulders tense. Finally, he sighs, a mix of frustration and reluctant acceptance in his expression. "I get it," he mutters, though his voice carries a note of hurt. "But it's still tough, you know? We've been working so hard for this."

Sunwoo nods, his throat tight. "I know. And I'm sorry. But I promise, this is something I have to do."

Miles rubs the back of his neck and offers a weak smile. "You're a good guy, Sunwoo. Just… make sure it's worth it."

"It is," Sunwoo replies, his voice steady now. And with that, the tension eases slightly, though the weight of their shared disappointment lingers. He explains the controls and strategy for the next rounds, urging Miles to compete without him.

Coming Home

The bus ride home feels endless. Sunwoo's mind churns with doubts. What if Miles loses without him? What if the judges think he's unreliable? What if he's forfeiting his one chance to achieve something extraordinary?

When he walks into the small apartment, though, all those worries fade. The familiar scent of his mother's jasmine tea mingles with the faint aroma of laundry detergent, and the soft hum of the old fridge fills the air. The walls, adorned with family photos and a slightly tilted calendar, seem to radiate a comforting warmth. Sunwoo's eyes catch the cluttered but cozy living room, where mismatched cushions and a worn-out blanket draped over the couch remind him of countless family movie nights. In this space, he feels grounded, his earlier doubts melting away into a sense of belonging. His mom looks up from the kitchen table, where she's folding laundry. Her normally tidy hair is in a messy bun, and dark circles rim her eyes.

"Sunwoo," she says, surprised. "You came home?"

"I'm here to help," he replies simply.

She stares at him for a moment, then pulls him into a hug. "Thank you."

Finding Purpose

The next hours are a blur of activity. Sunwoo helps Jiyeon prepare dinner while checking on their dad, who's resting fitfully in the bedroom. He runs to the pharmacy for medicine and takes over folding laundry so his mom can nap. Despite the chaos, there's a strange sense of calm in knowing he's exactly where he's needed.

Later, as the sun sets, Sunwoo sits by his father's bedside, holding a cool washcloth to his forehead. His father's eyes flutter open, and he gives a faint smile. "You should be at your competition," he murmurs, his voice raspy but kind.

Sunwoo hesitates, then replies softly, "I'll have other competitions. Right now, I need to be here."

His father's hand weakly reaches out, resting on Sunwoo's. "You've grown so much," he says, his words slow but heartfelt. "I'm proud of you, son."

In that moment, Sunwoo feels a swell of emotion—gratitude, determination, and love all rolled into one. He tightens his grip slightly, as if silently promising to carry their family through. The weight of his earlier doubts dissolves, replaced by a quiet confidence that he's made the right choice.

A New Opportunity

A week later, Sunwoo's back at school, and Miles catches up to him in the hallway. "Guess what?" Miles says, grinning. "We placed second. The judges were impressed with the design, and they want us to present at the state expo next month. Together."

Sunwoo's eyes widen. "Seriously?"

"Seriously," Miles replies. Then he punches Sunwoo lightly on the arm. "You're lucky I didn't mess it all up without you."

Sunwoo laughs. "Thanks, Miles. For understanding."

Miles shrugs. "What are friends for?"

That night, Sunwoo's mom places a hand on his shoulder as they sit at the dinner table. "I'm proud of you," she says. "For everything."

Her words warm him more than any trophy ever could. Sunwoo realizes that being a hero doesn't always mean winning competitions or saving the day in big, flashy ways. Sometimes, it's about being present when the situation demands it.

And for Sunwoo Park, that's the kind of hero he's proud to be.

The Day Sam Stood Tall

The Boy Who Dreamed of Heroes

Sam Harper is an ordinary 11-year-old boy with big brown eyes, curly black hair, and a mischievous smile that can light up a room—when he's not nervous, that is. He has a deep love for comic books, particularly those featuring superheroes who heroically intervene at the last moment. Sam often wonders what it would be like to be a hero, to stand up to his fears, and to finally confront the one thing that makes his heart pound and his palms sweat every single day—Tommy McGrath.

Tommy is the school bully, the kind that never runs out of mean tricks. A towering figure with a permanent scowl and a booming voice, Tommy has a way of making the bravest kids shrink back. For Sam, lunchtime is the worst part of the day. That's when Tommy likes to roam around the cafeteria like a lion looking for prey, knocking trays out of hands, making snide comments, and shoving kids out of his way. Sam's best friends, Raj and Diego, usually manage to dodge Tommy's path, but not Sam. No, it seems like Tommy has a special radar just for him.

A Turning Point

Today is no different. Sam sits with Raj and Diego at their usual table in the far corner of the cafeteria, near the window that looks out over the school playground. Sam likes this spot. It's safe and offers a great view of the large oak tree, which has been there longer than the school itself. He stares at the tree, imagining himself perched up there like his favorite superhero, watching over the city, ready to swing into action. Tommy's approach interrupts the thought, sending a familiar chill down his spine.

"Hey, Sammy the Scaredy Cat!" Tommy's voice booms across the cafeteria. Kids turn to watch; some giggle, and others look away, not wanting to be Tommy's next target. "What are you hiding today, huh? Got some of those peanut butter cookies again?"

Sam gulps. His mom packed his favorite peanut butter cookies today, but he knows better than to show any fear. He remembers the advice his dad once gave him: "Stand tall, Sam. Bullying feeds on fear." But that's easier said than done when you're staring up at Tommy, who seems twice his size.

"Leave him alone, Tommy," Raj says bravely, his small frame tensing up. Diego, who's usually quiet, nods in agreement.

Tommy's eyes narrow as he turns his attention to Raj. "Or what? You gonna stop me, Raj? With what, your math skills?"

Raj's face reddens, but he doesn't back down. "Yeah, maybe I will."

For a moment, Sam feels a spark of courage. Maybe today will be different. Maybe he won't have to be afraid. But then Tommy snatches the cookies from Sam's tray, crumples the bag in his fist, and crushes them to crumbs. The laughter from the tables nearby cuts through Sam's hopes.

Tommy grins and walks away, leaving Sam staring at the crushed cookies. It's not about the cookies, not really. It's about feeling powerless. He feels trapped in a cycle of fear and shame, even though he knows he should take action.

The Science Fair Plan

That night, lying in bed, Sam stares at his ceiling covered in glow-in-the-dark stars. He imagines himself as a hero again, someone who would never back down, not even from a giant like Tommy. His dad's words echo in his mind: "Stand tall, Sam." But how? What if standing tall just gets him flattened?

The next day at school, there's a buzz in the air. The annual science fair is coming up, and kids are excitedly discussing their projects. Raj is working on a homemade volcano, while Diego is building a solar-powered car. Sam, on the other hand, has no idea what to do. He's never been great at science, but he's got to come up with something.

"Hey, what if we make something that could help with... well, you know," Raj suggests, glancing around to make sure Tommy isn't within earshot.

"You mean a 'Stop Tommy' machine?" Diego jokes, but his eyes are serious.

"Yeah, like a superhero gadget," Sam adds, feeling a small flicker of hope. "Something that could help people who are scared."

They spend the lunch period brainstorming, sketching out ideas for a device that could alert kids when Tommy is near or maybe even record him bullying so they could show a teacher. They laugh at their wilder ideas—a force field, a robot assistant—but their excitement grows. The Hero Watch becomes their focus, though Sam's doubt lingers. What if it doesn't work? What if Tommy just smashes it?

By the end of the week, the trio has put together a prototype. They test it after school in Raj's garage. The watch vibrates successfully when Raj claps, but when Diego tries stomping, it buzzes twice. "It's hypersensitive," Raj mutters. "But maybe that's not so bad."

Standing Tall

On the day of the fair, the gymnasium is filled with colorful posters, bubbling beakers, and buzzing gadgets. Sam's group is tucked away in a corner, showcasing their "Hero Watch"— a bracelet that vibrates when it detects loud noises and movements typical of a bully approaching.

The watch isn't perfect; sometimes it goes off when someone drops a book or cheers too loudly. But it's a start. They feel proud, even hopeful. That is until Tommy and his friends approach their table.

"What's this junk?" Tommy sneers, eyeing the "Hero Watch." "You think this is gonna save you, Sammy?"

Raj starts to explain, but Tommy swipes the watch off the table and drops it to the floor, smashing it under his foot. The small crowd around them gasps. Sam feels the blood rush to his face, his heart pounding in his ears. He's worn out—tired of being scared, worn out of being the target, worn out of feeling small.

"Stop it, Tommy," Sam says, his voice shaking but louder than he expects. "Just stop."

The gym goes silent. Tommy freezes, looking at Sam with a mixture of surprise and amusement. "Or what, Sammy?" he mocks, stepping closer. "You gonna make me?"

Sam's knees tremble, but he forces himself to stand tall. "Yeah, I will."

Tommy laughs, a loud, booming sound that echoes through the gym, but Sam doesn't move. Something inside him shifts, like a lock clicking open. He realizes it's not about winning a fight—it's about showing everyone, including himself, that he's not afraid anymore.

Teachers start to notice the commotion and head over, but before they can intervene, something amazing happens. Raj and Diego step forward, standing beside Sam. Then, another kid joins them, and another. In seconds, a group of students forms around Sam, standing tall and united.

Tommy looks around, his smirk fading. He mutters something under his breath and, for the first time, backs away. The gym erupts into cheers.

A New Beginning

After that day, something changes at school. Tommy still glares at people and mutters under his breath, but his power isn't the same. Kids don't shrink away anymore. They've seen what standing together looks like. Sam becomes known as the kid who stood up, and he feels a new kind of confidence growing inside him, one that doesn't come from wishing he were someone else but from realizing he's enough just as he is.

Weeks later, as Sam climbs the branches of the big oak tree outside during recess, he feels the sun on his face and the wind in his hair. From up here, he can see everything—the school, the playground, the kids running and laughing. He smiles, feeling like a hero. This hero is not the one from comic books, but the genuine one—the one who rises to the occasion.

And for the first time, Sam realizes he doesn't need superpowers to be brave. He just needs to be himself.

From Backstage to Spotlight

A Reluctant Beginning

The school auditorium buzzes with nervous excitement as kids scurry around, costumes in hand and scripts tucked under their arms. Bright stage lights illuminate the half-finished set, where cardboard castles and glittering stars dangle precariously. In the midst of the controlled chaos stands Daniel Greyson, a quiet nine-year-old with a knack for noticing what others miss.

Daniel doesn't initiate the action by raising his hand first or sprinting to the front of the line. Instead, he's the type who watches from the sidelines, quietly absorbing everything around him. Daniel's calm demeanor and sharp attention to detail make him an unassuming yet invaluable presence when others falter. Daniel's reliability is evident in subtle, often unnoticed ways, whether he's helping a friend fix a broken prop or offering reassuring words. He consistently shows up when needed, stepping up when others fail to do so. However, he feels a sense of alienation today. The fifth-grade class play, Knights of the New Dawn, is just a week away, and Daniel's only role is manning the curtain. Daniel's role is not particularly heroic.

"Hey, Daniel," says Kai, a classmate with glasses too big for his small face. "Can you help me? My sword keeps falling apart."

Daniel crouches to inspect the foam sword Kai holds. "You need stronger tape," he says, grabbing duct tape from a nearby supply box. As he works, his gaze flickers to the stage. Amelia Carter, the lead actress, is rehearsing a scene. She delivers her lines perfectly, but her eyes dart nervously, as if she's unsure of her place.

"You're all set," Daniel says, handing the sword back to Kai. He's about to return to his corner when Ms. Alvarez, the drama teacher, claps her hands for attention.

The Call to Action

"We have a problem," she announces. "Liam's out with the flu, and he's our main knight. Without him, the whole play falls apart."

A ripple of murmurs spreads through the room. Daniel watches as Ms. Alvarez scans the group, her brow furrowed. "I need someone who can step in. Who knows Liam's lines?"

No hands go up. Daniel's stomach twists. Having witnessed Liam rehearse dozens of times, the lines have become ingrained in his memory. But what would it be like to step into the spotlight? That's terrifying.

Ms. Alvarez's eyes land on him. "Daniel, you're always paying attention. Can you do it?"

Daniel's mind races. He pictures himself fumbling the lines, tripping over his own feet, and the audience laughing. But then he thinks about the empty spotlight, the disappointed faces of his classmates, and the play falling apart. "I can't let them down," he thinks, his chest tightening with both fear and determination.

Every pair of eyes turns his way. His heart pounds. "I—I don't know," he stammers.

"We need you," Ms. Alvarez says gently. "You're our only hope."

Swallowing hard, Daniel nods. The room breaks into applause, but he feels anything but triumphant.

The Transformation

The following days are filled with intense activities. Daniel spends every lunch break practicing lines, sword-fighting moves, and blocking. Kai, Amelia, and their classmates rally around him, cheering him on and helping him rehearse. At first, his delivery is wooden, his movements are awkward. But slowly, with each stumble and correction, he improves.

Still, doubts gnaw at him. "What if I mess up?" he asks Amelia one afternoon. They're sitting on the edge of the stage, feet dangling.

Amelia smiles. "Everyone's nervous. I mean, I'm terrified I'll trip on my dress. But you know what? People are rooting for us. Just do your best, and it'll be amazing."

Her words comfort him, but a small voice in the back of his mind whispers, "You're not good enough."

Between rehearsals, Daniel discovers unexpected camaraderie. During a break, Kai unleashes a hilarious, exaggerated battle cry that sends both of them into fits of laughter. Another time, Amelia insists they all try her favorite tongue-twister warm-up, and everyone ends up tripping over their words and giggling uncontrollably. These moments of shared silliness help ease Daniel's nerves and forge a sense of team spirit that makes the whole experience unforgettable.

Opening Night

The night of the play arrives. Parents, siblings, and teachers fill the auditorium. Backstage, Daniel adjusts his costume—a tunic and a cardboard shield painted silver. The air smells of fresh paint and nervous sweat. Ms. Alvarez flits around, offering last-minute encouragement and fixing wayward props.

"Places!" Ms. Alvarez calls.

The curtain rises, and the play begins. Scene by scene, Daniel's confidence grows. However, midway through the second act, his cardboard shield slips out of his hand and clatters to the floor with a loud thunk. The audience gasps, causing Daniel to freeze momentarily. Then, without missing a beat, he grabs the shield, flashes a confident grin, and quips, "Even knights drop their shields sometimes!" The audience bursts into laughter, and Daniel's quick thinking earns him a wave of applause. The moment, though unexpected, cements his growing assurance on stage. His lines come out smoothly, his sword swings are precise, and he even improvises when another actor forgets a cue. The audience laughs, gasps, and claps in all the right places.

During intermission, Kai pats Daniel on the back. "You're crushing it," he says, grinning. "I'm glad you stepped up."

"Thanks," Daniel replies. "I couldn't have done it without you guys."

The Climax

Then comes the final scene. Daniel's character, the brave knight, faces off against the villain, played by Kai. It's the climax of the story, the moment the knight must choose between revenge and forgiveness.

"You took everything from me," Daniel says, his voice steady and strong. "But I won't become like you. I choose mercy."

The audience erupts into applause as Daniel extends a hand to Kai. The villain hesitates, then takes it, symbolizing a truce. It's a powerful moment, one that resonates with everyone watching.

A New Confidence

After the curtain falls, the cast huddles backstage, grinning and chattering. Ms. Alvarez gathers them for a quick speech. "You all were incredible," she says. "Daniel, you were instrumental in saving the day. Thank you for stepping up."

Daniel blushes but can't hide his smile. For the first time, he feels like he belongs, like he's part of something bigger than himself.

As the cast disperses, Amelia pulls Daniel aside. "Hey," she says, "you were amazing out there. You should try out for the next play."

Daniel laughs. "Maybe."

Walking home that night, Daniel thinks about the journey he's been on. He began his journey as the child hiding behind the curtain, feeling unnoticed and uncertain. Now, as he reflects on the night's events, Daniel realizes how far he's come. At first, the idea of stepping into the spotlight had felt impossible, a challenge meant for someone braver or more talented. But now, he sees that courage isn't about being fearless—it's about taking the first step despite the fear. He remembers the applause, the laughter, and the way his classmates had looked at him with pride. For the first time, Daniel feels truly seen, and the knowledge that he's capable of so much more fills him with a quiet determination.

The streetlights cast a warm glow on the sidewalk, and Daniel feels a sense of pride he's never known before. The cheers and laughter from the audience still echo in his mind, a reminder of what he's achieved.

When he reaches his front door, his mom greets him with a hug. "How was it?" she asks.

"Amazing," Daniel replies, beaming. "I can't wait to tell you everything."

That night, as he lies in bed, Daniel replays the events of the evening. He thinks about Kai, Amelia, Ms. Alvarez, and even Oliver. Each of them played a role in his success, proving that heroes don't act alone. They inspire, support, and grow together. With that thought, Daniel drifts off to sleep, dreaming of new adventures yet to come.

Team Innovate

The Challenge

The gym buzzes with energy as the seventh graders pile in, chatting loudly and jostling one another. Jackson Fields—all scuffed sneakers, tousled blond hair, and a confidence that only comes from scoring the most goals on the soccer team—leans against the bleachers, tossing a soccer ball in the air. It should be a routine class meeting today. There is no need for concern.

"Alright, settle down," calls Ms. Carroll, clapping her hands for attention. The students groan and shuffle to their seats, the energy dipping slightly. Jackson slumps next to his best friend, Cooper, ready to zone out.

But Ms. Carroll's next announcement has the whole room groaning louder.

"We're starting a school-wide competition," she says, smiling despite the wave of protests. Groans ripple across the room as students slump in their seats or exchange exasperated glances. For most, "competition" means extra work piled on top of already busy schedules, and the prospect of teamwork—often messy and frustrating—only makes it worse. A few brave souls whisper complaints about past competitions that went disastrously, while others, like Jackson, just sigh and tune out, assuming it'll be another chaotic mess. "Each homeroom will create a project that represents teamwork and innovation. Your team has to come up with a practical solution to a problem or an idea that makes life easier. And before anyone asks, yes, this is graded."

Jackson's heart sank. Science and school projects are not his thing. He'd rather be on the soccer field, perfecting his free kick. Ms. Carroll waves a hand for silence and continues, "I've already assigned teams."

The Team

Assigned teams? Jackson sits up, frowning. He exchanges a glance with Cooper, who whispers, "This is going to be bad."

Ms. Carroll begins to read names, and Jackson's frown intensifies when his name doesn't match Cooper's. "Jackson Fields," she says finally, "you'll be working with Ari Sharma and Sophie Williams."

"Who?" Jackson blurts before he can stop himself. The class laughs, but Ms. Carroll gives him a sharp look.

"Ari is new to our school, and Sophie is in the honors program. This is a great opportunity to make new friends," Ms. Carroll says pointedly.

Jackson groans inwardly as Ari stands, shyly adjusting his glasses and looking at the floor. He's skinny, with dark hair and a backpack that seems way too big for him. Sophie waves brightly, her curls bouncing as she flashes a grin. Jackson isn't sure which is worse: the shy new kid or the overachiever.

By lunch, Jackson has already decided the project's going to be a disaster. He finds Ari sitting alone at the edge of the cafeteria and plops his tray down across from him. Sophie arrives moments later, carrying a notebook and what looks like a color-coded planner.

"Okay, team," Sophie begins, setting her things down. "We've got two weeks to come up with an idea. Any thoughts?"

Jackson shrugs. "Can we just make a poster or something?" Jackson suggests, his voice tinged with reluctance. He knows bigger projects require effort and time—two things he'd rather spend on soccer. A poster feels simple, manageable, and, most importantly, quick. However, there's a nagging doubt and apprehension about taking on a more ambitious idea.

Sophie narrows her eyes. "A poster isn't innovative. It has to be creative and solve a problem." She turns to Ari. "What about you? Any ideas?"

Ari fidgets with the strap of his backpack. "Well, um, I'm into robotics. Maybe we could do something with that?"

"Robots?" Jackson snorts. "Yeah, because everyone's got a workshop in their garage."

Ari's face flushes, but he doesn't back down. Inside, he senses the familiar sting of undervaluation, yet he ignores it. He tightens his grip on his backpack strap and thinks of all the times he'd worked on projects alone, dreaming of moments like this where his ideas might actually matter. "It doesn't have to be complicated," he says quietly, determination settling into his voice like a steady rhythm. "I was considering a solution that could benefit athletes." Like a training robot."

Jackson raises an eyebrow. "Is there a robot for soccer? How would that even work?"

"It could help with drills," Ari says, warming to the idea. "It could be beneficial for tasks such as passing accuracy and goalkeeping practice. I've built simple bots before, so it's not impossible."

Sophie beams. "I love it! That's exactly the kind of creativity the judges are looking for."

Jackson isn't convinced, but he doesn't have a better idea. "Fine," he mutters. "But don't blame me when this blows up."

Building the Dream

The next two weeks are filled with intense activity. Ari sets up shop in Sophie's garage, which quickly becomes their headquarters. Jackson shows up reluctantly at first, but soon finds himself intrigued as Ari sketches out designs and explains how the robot will work.

"See?" Ari says one afternoon, pointing to a drawing. "The bot can pass the ball at different speeds. You just adjust the settings here."

"What about aiming?" Jackson asks, leaning over the table.

"That's the tricky part," Ari admits. "But I think I can program it to track movement."

Jackson admits it's kind of cool. He even volunteers to test the robot once Ari builds a prototype. But not everything goes smoothly. The first test ends with the bot flinging the ball into Sophie's mom's rose bushes, and another attempt sends the ball bouncing down the street.

"This is never going to work," Jackson grumbles after retrieving the ball for the third time.

Ari's shoulders slump, but Sophie steps in. "We just need to troubleshoot. It's part of the process."

"Easy for you to say," Jackson mutters. "You're not the one chasing soccer balls."

"Actually," Sophie says with a sly grin, "I think the bot needs more input data. Jackson, if you could run some drills while Ari records, we might be able to fix the issue."

Jackson groans but agrees. Over the next few days, he practices kicks and passes while Ari takes notes and adjusts the robot's programming. The bot gradually enhances its performance. One late afternoon, Ari makes a breakthrough by tweaking the motion sensors, enabling the robot to respond to Jackson's movements. Jackson kicks the ball, and the bot seamlessly intercepts it before passing it back with precise accuracy. Sophie cheers, clapping her hands. "It worked!" she exclaims. Ari grins, wiping sweat from his forehead. "I can't believe it," he says. "All the adjustments finally paid off." Jackson can't hide his excitement either, dribbling the ball and passing it to the robot again. "This is actually pretty awesome," he admits. The moment feels like a triumph, a pivotal moment where all their hard work culminates. By the final test, it's passing the ball with pinpoint accuracy.

The Competition

On the day of the competition, students, parents, and judges fill the gym. Jackson stands nervously by their table as Ari and Sophie set up the robot. The robot appears sleek, adorned in school colors and bearing the words "Team Innovate" across its front.

When the judges approach, Ari takes a deep breath and starts explaining their project. Sophie chimes in with statistics about teamwork and how their bot promotes inclusivity in sports. Jackson demonstrates the bot's features, kicking a perfect pass back and forth with the machine.

The judges nod, impressed, and Jackson feels a flicker of pride. Maybe this wasn't such a disastrous idea after all.

At the end of the day, their team doesn't win first place, but they take home the award for "Most Creative Solution." As they pose for a photo with their certificate, Jackson grins and claps Ari on the back.

"Not bad, robot genius," he says, a smile tugging at his lips. He remembers how he had dismissed the idea at first, certain it would fail. Now, standing here, he feels a surge of pride—not just in the robot, but in the team they'd become. It's remarkable how things can transform when given a chance.

Ari smiles shyly. "Thanks. Couldn't have done it without you."

Later, as they're packing up, Jackson turns to Ari. "Hey, have you ever thought about joining the soccer team? We could use someone who understands strategy."

Ari's eyes widen. "Me? On the soccer team?"

"Why not?" Jackson shrugs. "You've got the brains. And maybe I'll teach you a few tricks."

Ari hesitates, then nods. "Okay. But only if you help me with my next robotics project."

"Deal," Jackson says, grinning.

A New Beginning

As they leave the gym, Jackson realizes something. The competition wasn't just about winning or robots. It was about seeing things differently—about seeing people differently. And maybe—just maybe—he'd made some pretty great friends along the way.

As they walk to the parking lot, Sophie adds, "By the way, I was thinking about pitching the robot idea to the student council. Imagine if we could get funding to develop it further. Think about how many kids could benefit."

Jackson raises an eyebrow. "More funding? So, like, turning it into an actual training tool?"

Ari nods enthusiastically. "We could even add more features—like speed tracking or obstacle courses."

Jackson laughs. "You guys are serious about this, huh?"

Sophie grins. "Absolutely. Who knows? This could be just the beginning."

Ari looks at Jackson. "So, are you in?"

Jackson glances between them, then smirks. "Yeah, I'm in. Let's make this robot famous."

As they head off together, the bond between them feels stronger. What started as a random team assignment has become something much bigger. And Jackson realizes that sometimes stepping outside your comfort zone is exactly what you need to grow.

The Integrity Test

A Tempting Shortcut

The day begins with the sound of waves crashing outside
Kekoa's window. Kekoa Kainalu, at twelve years old, is
accustomed to the rhythm of life on his small Hawaiian
island, but today feels distinct. Today is the day of the history
exam—the one that could determine whether he earns a spot
in the advanced program next semester. For Kekoa, this
program represents more than just improving his academic
performance; it serves as a crucial step towards his
aspiration of becoming a marine biologist. The advanced
program would give him access to specialized resources, field
trips to marine research centers, and even opportunities to
meet scientists who study the ocean he loves so much. It feels
like everything he's worked for hinges on this moment, and
the weight of it presses on him. But he's nervous. Really
nervous.

As he slides his favorite blue hoodie over his school uniform, Kekoa takes a deep breath. His mom calls from the kitchen, "Don't forget your lunch, Kekoa! Spam musubi and an apple." He grins despite his jitters. "Thanks, Mom!"

When he arrives at school, the usual buzz of chatter feels heavier. Everyone's talking about the exam. His best friend, Jaylen, leans against the lockers, flipping through his notes. Jaylen is always cool under pressure, but today, even he looks tense.

"Hey, you ready?" Jaylen asks.

Kekoa shrugs. "Ready as I'll ever be. What about you?"

"Eh, sorta. But I heard something crazy," Jaylen whispers, glancing around. "Some kids got the answers."

Kekoa freezes. "Seriously?"

Jaylen nods. "I observed the trading papers this morning. It's risky, though. Mr. Nakamura's sharp. He'll catch anyone cheating."

Mr. Nakamura is their history teacher, known for his strictness but also his fairness. Kekoa can't imagine disappointing him. Still, the thought of those answers tempts him. What if he fails? What if this is his only shot at the advanced program?

As they enter the classroom, Kekoa notices Danny, a classmate who's always boasting about his high scores, slipping a folded piece of paper into his desk. Danny catches Kekoa's gaze and smirks. Kekoa quickly looks away.

A Test of Character

The exam begins, and the room falls silent except for the scratch of pencils on paper. Kekoa's heart pounds in his chest like the distant rhythm of a drum. He grips his pencil tightly, feeling the slickness of sweat on his palms. The faint smell of eraser shavings mixes with the distant hum of a lawnmower outside, but the sounds blur into the background. His mind races as he reads the first question—it's harder than he anticipated. He glances briefly at the clock, the tick of the second hand louder than ever. In the corner of his eye, he notices Danny shifting in his seat, a furtive glance cast toward his desk. Kekoa's stomach tightens, the weight of the room's tension pressing down on him.

Then he remembers something his grandfather told him while they were fishing last summer: "Integrity is like the ocean, Kekoa. Deep and steady. Remember when the tide was rough, and we had to be patient to reel in the fish? That patience and honesty are what define a good person. Even when the surface gets rough, it's what's beneath that matters." Kekoa had loved those fishing trips, the calm of the waves, and the wisdom his grandfather always shared. The memory strengthens his resolve, grounding him like the steady pull of the ocean's depths.

Kekoa takes a deep breath and focuses. He'll do this on his own, no matter what.

The Consequences of Cheating

Halfway through the test, Mr. Nakamura's voice cuts through the silence. "Danny, what's that?"

Everyone's heads snap up, their faces a mix of shock and curiosity. Some students exchange nervous glances, while others stare wide-eyed at Danny, their pencils frozen mid-sentence. A soft murmur ripples through the room as a few whisper to each other, but the atmosphere remains tense. Mr. Nakamura's words hang in the air, pressing down on everyone like a heavy blanket. Even Jaylen leans back in his chair, his brow furrowed as he watches the scene unfold, his usual confidence replaced with unease. Danny freezes, his face turning pale. Mr. Nakamura advances and retrieves the folded paper from Danny's desk. The silence fills the room.

"Cheating is a serious offense," Mr. Nakamura says, his voice calm but firm. "You'll need to come with me."

As Danny leaves the room, his head hung low, Kekoa feels a mix of relief and sadness. He knows Danny made a terrible choice, but he can't help but feel sorry for him. Still, Kekoa's determination solidifies. He finishes the test with everything he's got, pouring every ounce of focus into his answers.

Redemption and Friendship

The next day, Mr. Nakamura returned to their graded exams. Kekoa's hands tremble as he unfolds his paper. A "B+" stares back at him. It's not perfect, but it's good enough for the advanced program. Kekoa's face lights up with a smile.

After class, Mr. Nakamura pulls him aside. "Kekoa, I saw how you handled yourself during the test. It's not just your grade that impressed me. It's your character. You've got what it takes to succeed, not just here but in life."

Kekoa's chest swells with pride. As he leaves the classroom, he spots Danny in the hallway, looking dejected. Kekoa hesitates, then walks over.

"Hey, Danny," he says. "You okay?"

Danny looks up, surprised. "Not really. I blew it."

Kekoa nods. "Indeed, it's not a catastrophic event. You can bounce back from this. If you want, I can help you study for the next exam."

Danny blinks, then gives a small smile. "Thanks, Kekoa. That means a lot."

Over the next few weeks, Kekoa and Danny meet after school to study together. At first, it's awkward. Danny avoids eye contact and speaks in clipped sentences, clearly embarrassed by what happened. Kekoa, unsure how to bridge the gap, starts with simple questions. Slowly, Danny begins to open up, admitting that he struggles with dates and connecting events.

They create flashcards and quiz each other, and as the days pass, their sessions become more animated. Kekoa finds himself explaining concepts with excitement, using vivid examples from Hawaiian history to make the lessons stick. Danny, in turn, shares tricks he's learned for memorizing facts, and they laugh over their mistakes. When the next exam arrives, Danny is prepared and confidently enters the classroom.

The Ripple Effect of Integrity

When the results come back, Danny beams at his "B," and Kekoa's grin matches his. The experience cements their friendship and shows the whole school that honesty and hard work truly pay off. Other students begin to talk about what happened, sharing how Kekoa's example made them think twice about their own choices. Teachers notice the shift in the classroom, with more students taking their work seriously and showing support for one another. Kekoa's quiet leadership fosters a sense of trust and respect, proving that one act of integrity can ripple outward and make a difference. And though he doesn't seek recognition, he's proud to be known as the boy who stayed true to himself, no matter the odds.

The Knight's Journey

Betrayal in the Cafeteria

Ten-year-old Zayd Khatib grips the straps of his backpack tightly as he walks into the school cafeteria. The hum of chatter and clinking trays fills the air. Zayd's heart thuds in his chest, louder than the noise around him. He scans the tables, searching for his best friend, Elijah Morales. A wave of relief washes over him when he spots Elijah's curly head in the corner. Elijah is laughing, surrounded by a group of kids.

Zayd weaves through the crowded room, his sneakers squeaking on the tile floor. As he approaches, Elijah glances up. The laughter at the table grows louder, and Zayd's relief twists into confusion. One of the kids, a boy named Ben, smirks.

"Hey, Zayd," Ben calls out. "Is it true you're scared of the dark?"

Zayd freezes. Heat rushes to his face, and his grip on his backpack tightens. He looks at Elijah, hoping for an explanation, but his friend avoids his gaze, focusing on the apple in his hand.

"What's the big deal?" Ben continues. "Elijah told us you sleep with a nightlight."

The table erupts in giggles. A sharp, hollow ache spreads through Zayd's chest like a punch. His mind races with questions: Why would Elijah betray him like this? Why did it have to happen here, in front of everyone? He feels the sting of humiliation, as though the entire cafeteria is laughing at him, not just the kids at the table. His face burns, and the words he wants to say are stuck in his throat, swallowed by the knot of hurt and anger tightening inside him. That secret was something he'd only ever shared with Elijah during a sleepover last month. Elijah had promised to keep it between them.

Without a word, Zayd turns and walks away. He can feel their eyes on him, the laughter echoing in his ears. He doesn't stop until he reaches the empty stairwell near the library. He sinks onto the bottom step, hugging his knees to his chest. The cold concrete presses against him, grounding him slightly as he takes deep breaths, trying to steady his thoughts. Anger and embarrassment churn inside him, an uncomfortable mix that he doesn't know how to handle.

A Quiet Escape

For the rest of the day, Zayd avoids Elijah. In class, he keeps his head down, scribbling in his notebook. During recess, he hides behind the shed near the soccer field, pretending to be engrossed in a book. The shed smells faintly of grass and old wood, and though it's not comfortable, it's a safe escape. The quiet here feels like a shield against the noise of the world, a place where Zayd can think without interruption. It reminds him of building forts with his cousins back home, a time when he felt secure and in control. Even though the shed is cold and cramped, it's his refuge, offering a small sense of peace in the chaos of the day. By the time the final bell rings, he feels a heavy mix of sadness and anger swirling inside him.

"Zayd, wait up!" Elijah's voice calls as they leave the school building. Zayd quickens his pace, but Elijah jogs to catch up. "Hey, I'm sorry. I didn't think it was a big deal."

Zayd stops abruptly and turns to face him. "Not a big deal? You promised, Elijah. That was supposed to stay between us!" The slight crack in his voice reveals the depth of his hurt.

Elijah frowns, shoving his hands into his pockets. "I didn't mean to hurt you. Ben was just joking around, and it slipped out. I... I messed up, okay?"

"Yeah, you did." Zayd's voice trembles. "How can I trust you now?"

Elijah opens his mouth to reply, but Zayd shakes his head and walks away. He doesn't look back, even when he hears Elijah mutter a soft "I'm sorry" behind him.

The Knight Takes Shape

At home, Zayd's mom notices his silence during dinner. "Everything okay, habibi?" She inquires gently, her dark eyes brimming with concern.

He shrugs, pushing his rice around on the plate. "Just tired," he mutters. His mom's comforting hand on his shoulder makes him feel a pang of guilt, but he's not ready to talk about it yet.

That night, as he lies in bed, the faint glow of his nightlight casts soft shadows on the wall. He's too upset to fall asleep, replaying the betrayal over and over in his mind. Eventually, he grabs his sketchpad and starts to draw. It's his safe space, where he can pour out his feelings. His pencil moves furiously, creating a scene of a knight standing alone, his shield cracked and his sword broken. The jagged lines and stormy background reflect the betrayal he feels, the isolation cutting deep. The knight, so clearly modeled after himself, stares ahead with a mixture of hurt and determination.

Zayd's hand falters for a moment as he wonders if the knight will ever repair his shield or if it will always bear the marks of betrayal.

A Test of Courage

The next morning, Zayd's mom surprises him with a stack of pancakes. "Whatever's bothering you, you'll figure it out," she says with a kiss on his forehead. "You always do." Her unwavering confidence in him gives him a small spark of hope.

At school, Zayd is determined to avoid Elijah again. But during art class, their teacher, Mr. Reynolds, pairs them together for a group project. They're supposed to design a poster about teamwork.

"Great," Zayd mutters under his breath as Elijah slides into the chair next to him. They work in tense silence for a while. Elijah glances at Zayd's sketch of a soccer team celebrating a win.

"That's really good," Elijah says.

Zayd doesn't respond, focusing on adding details to the players' jerseys. He's pouring all his frustration into the art, making the lines sharper and more precise than usual.

Finally, Elijah sighs. "Look, I know I hurt you. I've been thinking about it all night, and I feel terrible. What can I do to make it right?"

Zayd pauses, his pencil hovering over the paper. He's not sure what to say. He's still angry, but he can see that Elijah is genuinely sorry. Before he can answer, the bell rings, signaling lunch.

In the cafeteria, Zayd sits at the edge of a different table, away from Elijah and their usual group. As he picks at his sandwich, he overhears a commotion near the trash cans. Ben is there, teasing a younger boy who's struggling to carry a heavy science project.

"Careful, you might drop it," Ben sneers, pretending to trip the boy. The project wobbles dangerously.

Zayd's heart pounds. He hates confrontation, but something inside him pushes him to his feet. "Hey, Ben, leave him alone!" He calls out, his voice firmer than he feels.

Ben turns, raising an eyebrow. "What's it to you, nightlight boy?"

The cafeteria falls silent. Zayd's cheeks burn, but he squares his shoulders, forcing himself to stand tall. His heart pounding, he briefly contemplates retreating. But then he remembers how he felt earlier, sitting alone on the cold stairwell, and a surge of determination pushes him forward. His voice trembles at first, but he steadies it, refusing to let Ben see his fear. At that moment, Zayd isn't just defending the younger boy—he's standing up for himself, too. "Everyone has something they're afraid of. At least I don't pick on kids to make myself feel better."

For a moment, Ben looks stunned. Then he snorts and walks away. The younger boy mumbles a quick "Thanks" before scurrying off.

Zayd sits back down, his hands trembling. Across the room, he sees Elijah watching him with an expression Zayd can't quite read.

Forgiveness Takes Root

After school, Elijah catches up to him. "That was awesome," he says. "You were really brave."

Zayd shrugs. "I just did what I thought was right."

Elijah hesitates. "Can I say something?"

Zayd nods warily.

"You're right to be upset at me. I broke your trust, and I'll do whatever it takes to earn it back. But seeing you stand up to Ben today reminded me why you're my best friend. You're a better person than I am."

Zayd looks at him, surprised. Elijah's words feel sincere, and for the first time since the betrayal, the tight knot in Zayd's chest loosens a little.

"I'm still mad," Zayd admits. "But I don't want to stay upset forever."

Elijah's face lights up with a hopeful smile. "Does that mean we're okay?"

Zayd thinks for a moment. "Not yet. But maybe we can start over." As the words leave his mouth, he reflects on what forgiveness means. Forgiving Elijah doesn't mean forgetting what happened, but it's about giving his friend a chance to make things right. He realizes that holding onto anger only weighs him down, and he wants to move forward, not just for Elijah, but for himself too.

"I'll take it," Elijah says, holding out his fist. Zayd bumps it lightly, a small smile tugging at the corners of his mouth.

That night, Zayd sits at his desk, staring at the drawing of the lone knight. He picks up his pencil and adds a second figure beside the knight, holding a new shield. Together, they look ready to face anything. Around them, he sketches sunlight breaking through the storm clouds, a symbol of hope and healing.

As he clicks off his desk lamp and crawls into bed, Zayd feels lighter. Forgiving Elijah doesn't erase the hurt, but it's a step toward something better. And maybe—just maybe—it's the start of a stronger friendship.

A Night to Remember

Pre-Show Jitters

The school auditorium buzzes with energy as banners hang from the walls, colorful stage props await their turn in the spotlight, and kids scurry around in costumes, rehearsing their lines. But for 9-year-old Noah Littlefeather, the excitement is drowned out by the weight in his chest. Tonight, is the annual talent showcase, and for the first time, he's performing a traditional Lakota song on his cedar flute in front of the entire school. His mother had called it a way to share his heritage with pride. Noah, however, just wishes he could disappear.

He's not alone. His best friend, Omar, a cheerful boy with a knack for beatboxing, claps Noah on the back. "You've got this," Omar says, trying to lend some of his confidence. "That flute of yours can make people feel things. You'll crush it."

Noah forces a smile. "Sure, if I don't mess up." He glances at his hands, fingers trembling slightly.

A sharp voice interrupts their conversation: "Noah, stop daydreaming. We need you to carry props backstage!" It's Tara, the show's student director. Always bossy but efficient, she's determined to keep everything on schedule.

Noah grabs a set of fake rocks, his hands gripping them tightly as a wave of nervous energy washes over him. The weight of the props feels insignificant compared to the knot in his stomach, a constant reminder of the daunting performance ahead. He forces himself to take steady steps toward the backstage area, each one feeling heavier than the last. On his way, he passes a group of younger kids practicing their dance routine. Among them is Jamal, a second-grader who always looks up to Noah. "You're going to be amazing tonight," Jamal says with a gap-toothed grin. Noah nods, but the knot in his stomach tightens.

A Flute's Story

As Noah reaches backstage, a new problem arises. The sound system's acting up. Ms. Harper, the teacher in charge, looks frazzled as she fiddles with wires. "It's not picking up the microphones," she mutters. "This could delay the entire show."

"I can help," offers Javier, a tech-savvy classmate. But the tension is palpable. Noah places the props down and quietly steps away, not wanting to add to the chaos.

He ducks outside for a moment to catch his breath. The crisp evening air fills his lungs, carrying the faint scent of pine and damp earth. He pulls out the cedar flute from his backpack, its smooth wood gleaming under the dim light of the parking lot. As he runs his fingers along the intricate carvings, memories of his grandfather flood his mind. "This flute carries our stories," Grandpa had said, his voice steady and full of pride. Noah inhales deeply, allowing the weight of those words to subside. He wonders if he's ready to honor those stories or if the pressure will break him.

Noah raises the flute to his lips, but before he can play, the door bangs open. His older sister, Maya, steps out, her arms crossed. "Still doubting yourself?" she asks, her tone both teasing and concerned.

"Maybe," Noah admits. "What if they laugh? Or don't understand?"

Maya softens. "They'll feel what you feel. That's the magic of it. Besides, Mom and Dad are counting on you to show everyone what we're about."

Noah groans. "No pressure, right?"

Maya laughs, then pats his shoulder. "You'll be great. Now, come back in. All hands must be available."

Overcoming Obstacles

Back inside, chaos reigns. The microphone issue escalates as the clock ticks closer to showtime. Tara paces nervously while Ms. Harper makes frantic phone calls. Noah spots Omar trying to cheer up a nervous performer who forgot her lines. Javier crouches over the soundboard nearby, scattering wires everywhere. He shakes his head. "I think it's fried," he says grimly.

Tara murmurs, "We're in trouble. "The entire show would collapse without the sound." system. "Not necessarily," Noah says, surprising even himself. Everyone turns to look at him. "I mean, we could go without microphones. It'd be harder to hear, but... maybe it'll feel more... real?"

Tara's skeptical, but Ms. Harper nods. "That might work. Let's get everyone to project their voices. And Noah—thanks for stepping up."

Noah feels a small spark of pride, but it's short-lived as the first act begins. He watches from the wings as performers brave the stage without the safety net of amplification. Despite the challenges, the audience seems engaged. Omar's beatboxing act brings roaring applause, and Jamal's group earns cheers for their spirited dance. The younger kids stumble a bit but recover with enthusiasm, earning chuckles and encouraging applause from the crowd.

A Hero's Performance

Finally, it's Noah's turn. As he steps onto the stage, the spotlight feels blinding, casting a sharp cone of light that makes the rest of the auditorium fade into darkness. The murmurs of the audience hush abruptly, replaced by an almost tangible silence filled with anticipation. Noah can hear the faint rustle of papers and the occasional cough, each sound amplified in the stillness. His heart pounds in his chest, and he wonders if everyone can hear it echoing. The expectant faces in the crowd blur together, but the warmth of his family's smiles in the front row anchors him. Clutching the flute, he closes his eyes and takes a deep breath. He imagines his grandfather's encouraging smile and his family sitting in the front row, their expressions filled with hope.

Noah begins to play. The first notes are shaky, his fingers fumbling slightly as nerves try to take over. But then, he remembers his grandfather's words, and he focuses on the melody, letting it guide him. The tune begins to flow; each note more confident than the last. As he plays, a calm washes over him, and the music feels alive, telling a story not just of his heritage but also of his journey tonight. The haunting, soulful tune becomes an extension of his emotions, weaving strength, love, and gratitude into the air.

As the melody continues, Noah's confidence grows. He opens his eyes and sees the audience leaning forward, captivated. He spots Jamal swaying to the music and Omar nodding along with a proud grin. Even Tara looks impressed, her clipboard forgotten at her side. The final note hangs in the air, resonating with a deep, emotional weight.

Gratitude and Growth

When he finishes, there's a moment of silence before the auditorium erupts in applause. Noah opens his eyes to see smiles and even a few tears in the crowd. His parents beam with pride, and Omar gives him a thumbs-up from the wings. Jamal's enthusiastic cheering makes Noah laugh.

After the show, students and parents gather to congratulate the performers. Jamal runs up to Noah and says, "You were awesome! I want to play the flute like you someday!"

Noah kneels down. "You can do anything if you practice and believe in yourself," he says, ruffling Jamal's hair. "And maybe I can teach you sometime," he adds with a wink.

Maya and his parents join him, their pride is evident. "You showed everyone who you are tonight," his mom says, pulling him into a hug.

"And you reminded me why it's important," Noah replies. "Thank you for always believing in me."

As they leave the school, Noah feels lighter. The applause was nice, but it's the warmth of his family's support and the realization of how much he has to be grateful for that fills him with true joy. He glances at his flute, a symbol of not just his heritage but also the love and encouragement that helped him find his voice.

At that moment, Noah knows this is just the beginning. Whatever challenges lie ahead, he'll face them with courage, gratitude, and the melodies that carry his story. He glances at his family, their proud smiles reminding him of the countless ways they've supported him. The applause is a momentary thrill, but it's their belief in him that truly gives him strength. With their love as his foundation, Noah feels ready to embrace whatever lies ahead. As they walk to the car, Omar catches up and says, "Next year, we should perform together. Beatboxing and flute—what do you think?"

Noah laughs. "Sounds like a plan." His sister chimes in, "And I'll choreograph it. We'll make it unforgettable."

Noah looks at his family and friends, the people who make him feel brave even when he's scared. "Yeah," he says with a smile. "Unforgettable."

The Shot of a Lifetime

A Game-Changing Moment

The gym buzzes with energy as the crowd's cheers echo through the rafters. Connor O'Rourke, an eight-year-old with fiery red hair and a sprinkle of freckles across his nose, tightens his grip on the basketball. He's small for his age, but what he lacks in size, he makes up for in determination. The clock above the scoreboard ticks ominously—forty-five seconds to go, the score tied at 34.

Connor's heart pounds as he glances at the stands. His dad gives him a thumbs-up, his rugged hands cupped around his mouth as if to shout encouragement, while his mom offers a reassuring smile, her eyes gleaming with pride. Connor's throat tightens as he imagines their hopes resting on him. The weight of their expectations presses down like a heavy fog. What if he messes up? What if he lets everyone down? His mind churns with doubt, but beneath it all, a tiny ember of determination sparks. This is his moment, and he is aware that he must confront it directly, despite the potential for his nerves to overwhelm him. The roar of the crowd feels distant, muffled by the pounding in his ears, and for a moment, the smells of popcorn and freshly polished gym floors seem sharper than the cheers. He wipes his palms on his shorts, inhaling deeply to steady his racing thoughts. "Focus," he tells himself, clinging to the words like a lifeline.

Journey to the Court

His coach calls a time-out, and the team huddles together. "Alright, guys," Coach Miller says, his voice steady but firm. "We've worked hard for this. Trust your instincts, play as a team, and whatever happens, know you've done your best."

Connor nods, though a lump forms in his throat. The pressure is overwhelming. It's not just the game; it's everything leading up to this moment. As an introvert, Connor has always preferred the quiet of his room, sketching designs for robots or reading about historic explorers. His dad suggested basketball as a means to help Connor overcome his shyness. Despite initial resistance, Connor initially struggled to find his footing in basketball. He was unsure of himself, overwhelmed by the fast pace of the game, and intimidated by the energy of his more confident teammates. Practices were filled with missed shots and moments where he doubted whether he belonged on the court.

Connor still vividly remembers one practice when he tripped over his own feet while attempting a layup, sending the ball bouncing across the court. His teammates laughed, not out of cruelty but surprise, and Connor's cheeks burned with embarrassment. He had wanted to walk off the court and never return, but Coach Miller had pulled him aside, placed a reassuring hand on his shoulder, and said, "Mistakes are just part of getting better, Connor. Every player out here has had moments like that. Don't let one stumble stop you from improving." That encouragement had stuck with him, slowly chipping away at his self-doubt and pushing him to keep trying, even when things felt impossible.

Over time, as he honed his skills and embraced the challenge, a revelation occurred. He discovered a love for the rhythm of the game, the intricate strategies that played out like puzzles to be solved, and the unspoken bond that formed with his teammates. Gradually, basketball transformed from a mere sport into a profound passion.

The Final Play

"Connor, you'll take the inbound pass," Coach Miller says, snapping him back to the present. Connor's stomach churns as the words sink in. This is it—the moment the team is counting on him. Sweat slicks his palms, and for a fleeting moment, he contemplates delegating the task to someone else. But then he catches Marcus's encouraging grin and feels a flicker of courage. He nods resolutely, his hands tightening around the ball as he steps into position, determination settling over his nerves like a steadying hand.

The team claps and breaks the huddle. The energy is electric, a mixture of anticipation and nerves. Connor positions himself on the sideline, clutching the ball. His best friend, Marcus, a fast and fearless point guard, gives him a quick nod. Marcus, with his electric energy and ever-present grin, has been Connor's anchor through the season. DeShawn, the tallest player on the team, stands beside Marcus, always providing a kind word and a steady hand. On the other side, Sophie, their sharpshooter, adjusts her headband. Her focus is incredibly sharp. She is the team's hidden asset, consistently prepared to deliver when it matters most.

The referee sounds the whistle. Connor scans the court, searching for an open teammate. He spots Marcus, but an opponent blocks the lane. Sweat trickles down Connor's forehead. The crowd roars, and his hands tremble. Suddenly, Sophie breaks free. Connor takes a deep breath, plants his feet, and throws the ball. It soars through the air and lands perfectly in Sophie's hands. The crowd erupts in cheers.

Sophie dribbles down the court, weaving through defenders with practiced ease. The opposing team's defense is relentless, but Sophie's determination shines. She passes to DeShawn, who spins around his defender and shoots. The ball bounces off the rim. Marcus leaps for the rebound, catching it mid-air and dribbling back out. There are twenty seconds remaining.

"Connor!" Marcus shouts, tossing the ball to him. Connor catches it, his mind racing. The defenders close in, their sneakers squeaking on the polished floor. Connor feels the weight of the game on his shoulders. "You got this, man!" Marcus calls out.

Connor remembers his dad's advice from their backyard practice sessions: "When the pressure's high, focus on what you can control. Breathe, visualize, and take your shot." Those words had guided him through countless moments of self-doubt, from struggling to make his first basket to overcoming the fear of letting his teammates down. Now, standing at the edge of the biggest moment of his young life, Connor clings to that advice, letting it anchor him. It's not just about basketball anymore; it's about proving to himself that he can rise above the chaos and find clarity when it matters most.

Connor exhales slowly, blocking out the noise. He dribbles to the right, feints left, and slips past his defender. Ten seconds. He's at the three-point line. The clock ticks louder in his mind. He glances at the hoop, its orange rim glaring back at him. He knows this shot will define the game.

He jumps, releasing the ball just as a defender lunges toward him. Time seems to freeze. The ball arcs high, spinning through the air. The crowd catches its breath. Connor lands on his feet, watching as the ball hits the backboard and drops into the net. The gym erupts in deafening cheers. The buzzer sounds. Connor's team wins, 37-34.

Victory and Growth

His teammates rush to him, lifting him off the ground. Marcus punches the air. "That's my guy!" he shouts. Sophie grins, giving Connor a high-five, while DeShawn pats him on the back. Connor's heart swells with pride. For the first time, he feels like he truly belongs. Their coach claps from the sidelines, shouting words of encouragement as the team revels in their victory.

As the team celebrates, Connor notices the opposing team's captain, Ethan, sitting on the bench, his head in his hands. Ethan's shoulders slump, and he draws a shaky breath, clearly trying to hold back tears. Connor hesitates for a moment, then walks over, extending a hand. "Good game," Connor says, his voice steady but kind. Ethan looks up, surprise flickering in his eyes before he takes Connor's hand. "Thanks," Ethan murmurs, managing a faint smile. "You played really well, too." The exchange lingers for a moment longer as Ethan straightens up slightly, the burden of defeat easing just a little. Connor claps him gently on the shoulder, and they part ways, united briefly by mutual respect for the game they both love. Connor glances back and sees Ethan sit a little straighter, his earlier despair replaced by a quiet determination. Connor wonders if Ethan's team will come back even stronger next time, and the thought fills him with respect and anticipation for their next meeting. This game brings out the best in everyone, even when you lose.

A Lesson Beyond Basketball

Later, as Connor walks out of the gym with his parents, his dad places a hand on his shoulder. "I'm proud of you, kiddo," he says. "Not just for the shot, but for how you handled yourself."

Connor smiles. The victory isn't just about the game. It's about learning to trust himself, to manage his anxiety, and to stay calm under pressure. Connor realizes that the ability to stay composed doesn't end on the basketball court. Whether it's facing a tough math test, presenting in front of the class, or navigating the ups and downs of friendships, this moment has taught him that clarity and focus can guide him through any challenge. Connor thinks about the upcoming science project he's dreading—a group assignment where he'll need to present in front of the whole class. Just imagining it had made his stomach churn last week, but now, he feels a flicker of confidence. If he can handle the pressure of a game-winning shot, maybe he can face that, too. One step at a time, he tells himself. The lesson feels more significant than the game, shaping him in ways he's just beginning to comprehend. He is aware that he will face additional challenges in the future, but tonight, he has demonstrated to himself that he can rise to the challenge.

In the car ride home, the conversation shifts from the game to life lessons. "So, how did it feel in that moment?" his mom asks. Connor hesitates, searching for the right words. "It felt...like everything slowed down," he says finally. "I just focused on what I had to do. I didn't let the noise get to me."

His dad smiles knowingly. "That's a lesson that goes beyond basketball, Connor. You'll find moments like that at school, in life, and everywhere. Just remember this feeling."

As they drive home, Connor gazes out the window, a small smile playing on his lips. He can still hear the cheers and feel the weight of the basketball in his hands. The image of his teammates celebrating and the pride in his parents' eyes stays with him. For the first time, he believes in his own strength. And that's a victory that will last far beyond the game.

Epilogue

Hey there, young reader.

By now, you've met boys like Timmy, Miguel, Sunwoo, and so many others. Perhaps you've even seen a bit of yourself in their stories. Whether it was Timmy standing up to bullies, Miguel leading his team to victory, or Sunwoo balancing dreams and family, each one faced challenges that seemed bigger than they were. But here's the thing: being a hero doesn't mean having superpowers. It involves taking the initial courageous step, even when your heart is thumping.

Every day, you have the chance to be someone's hero. It might be as simple as helping a classmate who's struggling with homework, standing up for what's right, or trying something that scares you. Those little moments add up, shaping you into someone who's not just strong but also kind, thoughtful, and true to yourself.

So, what's next for you? Maybe today is your day to try something new, like joining a team or sharing an idea you've been keeping to yourself. Or maybe you'll stand up for someone who needs a friend. Whatever you choose, remember: the courage to act starts with believing in yourself.

This book is filled with tales of boys who found their courage and made a difference. Now it's your turn. The world is full of adventures waiting for someone just like you to step up.

So, what kind of hero will you be?

The next story is yours to write.

Thank You for Being a Hero!

Wow, you did it! You've just finished *INSPIRELAND: School Stories of Everyday Boy Heroes*. I hope you had as much fun reading these stories as I did writing them. I created each story to serve as a reminder that heroes exist everywhere, including YOU.

As the author, I want to thank you for taking this adventure with me. You are the reason these stories come to life. If you enjoyed the book, I'd love to hear your thoughts!

Leaving a review is like giving the book a high-five—it shows others why they should check it out. Here's how you can do it:

- Ask a parent or guardian to help you visit the book's page on Amazon.

- Click "Write a review" and share what you liked most about the stories.

Did you have a favorite hero? Or maybe you found something in the book that reminded you of yourself?

Your review helps other kids discover *INSPIRELAND* and join the journey to becoming everyday heroes too!

Thank you for being amazing and for reading *INSPIRELAND*! I can't wait to hear about how these stories inspired you.

Your friend,
Grace Ann Grow

Keep dreaming big, standing tall, and being a hero every day!

LEAVE A REVIEW ON AMAZON:

United States	Canada	United Kingdom

Australia	India	Singapore

Printed in Dunstable, United Kingdom

66954983R00060